WE ALL ENJOY SPECIAL FRIENDS WITH

WHOM WE CAN SHARE ALL OUR

DREAMS AND FEARS

Charlotte,
DReam Big!
Tina Cole Kreitz

Chris Harper Triplett

Requests for permission to make copies of any part of the work should be submitted online at info@mascotbooks.com or mailed to Mascot Books, 560 Herndon Parkway #120, Herndon, VA 20170.

PRT0813A

Printed in the United States

Library of Congress Control Number: 2012952795

ISBN-13: 9781620861325
ISBN-10: 1620861321

www.mascotbooks.com

ROCKY THE SEA TURTLE

Tina Cole Kreitz

Illustrated by Chris Harper Triplett

On a cloudless day with bright sunshine and sparkling blue water, I was walking along my favorite beach on the island of Oahu in Hawaii. My brain was charging, racing, full of ideas I wanted to explore. I wanted a change. I wanted some magic in my life. I wanted to be daring.

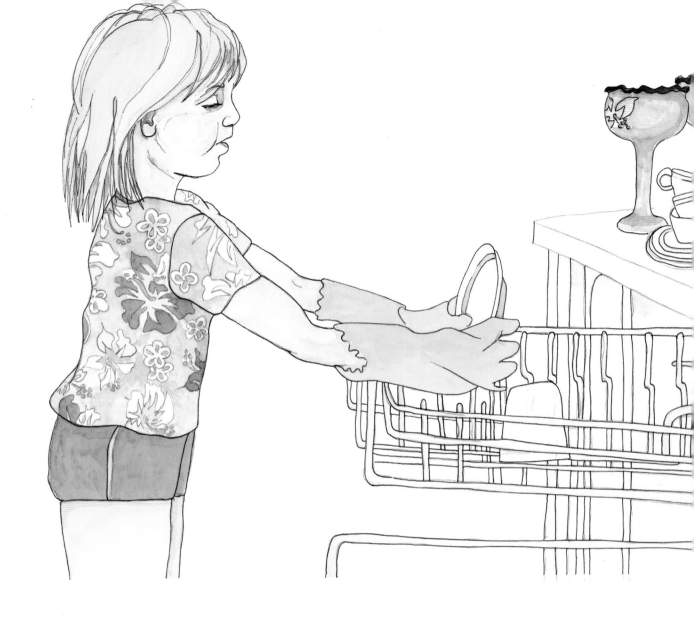

I am a good girl. I do my chores.
I am nice to my sister.

Well, most of the time, I am nice
and share with her.

I read, do my homework, and I am a good friend. I think I am boring.

I wanted to give my life a blast of color and pizzazz.

I walked along the beach, dancing in and out of the water as the waves came ashore.

I tried to think of what I would do differently.

Then I noticed something up on the shore by the lifeguard stand.

It looked like a sea turtle. I walked up the sandy beach to inspect, to get a closer look. This was not a normal green sea turtle. It was a turtle made of rocks. I bent down to look carefully at this rock creation.

Maybe one of the lifeguards made the turtle. Whoever did this, carefully selected each rock for size, shape, and color. Some reflected the sun, some were worn smooth by years of rolling in and out with the ocean waves, some could fit in my hand, and a few were too big to hold in my arms.

This creation was beautiful.

I knelt in the warm sand, very close to the rock turtle. I wanted to study the shape and try to figure out how I could copy it and make one in my garden. As I got eye-to-eye with the rock turtle's face, a rock eye blinked at me!

My eyes grew wide and I jumped up on my feet faster than a rabbit. I looked at the turtle with confusion, sure the sun made me see things that weren't real.

But even as I stood tall, looking down, the rock eyes opened and moved.

"Oh my! Holy Toledo! Is this magic? Is this a sign? What else will this turtle do?" I asked myself.

As I began to back away, I kept looking at the rocks. The turtle's eyes were following me!

Once I reached the walking path,
I ran home as fast as I could.

When I got home I pushed open
the door, calling for my mom.
"Mom, the rock turtle blinked its
eye at me!" I yelled.

Mom was in the kitchen. She looked puzzled. "How can a rock blink? Are you sure it wasn't your imagination?"

"Mommy, it's real. Come see."

"Oh, sweetie, I have to finish fixing dinner."

My grandmother was visiting and she came into the kitchen to find out what the excitement was about. I told her about the blinking-eye rock turtle.

Grandmother sat in our big, cozy chair and opened her arms for me to climb in her lap.

She said, "Aleka, tell me again about this rock turtle." I told her what I told Mom. She listened very seriously. I know she heard me. I know she believed me.

Grandmother told me she would like to see my rock turtle and maybe have a chance to talk to the turtle.

Grandmother and I made a plan. After dinner we would walk back to Sunset Beach to check on my rock turtle. I was so glad she was coming with me. I ate quickly. I wanted to make sure it was still light when I took Grandmother to Sunset Beach.

We held hands as we walked the path. I kept telling Grandmother to hurry. My heart was pounding. My feet were moving swiftly. My turtle had to be there, waiting.

We got to the beach and I slowed down. The lifeguards were just leaving their posts. They were laughing with each other and didn't notice me watching. I wanted them to leave so I could check on my rock turtle.

Finally, they walked away and I looked up at Grandmother. She smiled and nodded her head. I took her hand again and led her to the spot. And my rock turtle was there, waiting.

I got low, kneeling in the sand. I checked each rock, still all there.

I showed Grandmother the eye that winked at me. She knelt down and studied the rock eye. Slowly, the rock eye opened. Grandmother smiled and began to talk to my turtle. She sang it soothing songs. She touched its rock back.

She placed her wrinkled hand on the rock turtle head. "Oh, Honu, you beautiful being. You have come to tell us something special, I feel. What is it, rocky one? What are we to learn from you?"

My eyes popped wide open for the second time that day. Grandmother was talking in Hawaiian to my rock turtle!

She patted the rocks. She believed the magic. She shared my secret.

The turtle began to lift her head. The rocky head really moved! She looked at Grandmother.

My rock turtle was coming to life. It had to be magic.

The turtle began to move toward the water. Rocky Turtle could only move slowly over the sand, using her flippers to help her push her way forward.

Grandmother and I crawled along the sand with Rocky Turtle, watching her movements in wonder that she was really moving.

When we three got to the water, Rocky Turtle pushed herself into the waves.

Once in the water, my turtle was so graceful. She floated. She dove. She rode the waves.

And she used her flipper to tell us to come join her in the warm water.

She let us ride on her back as she dove under the waves. We held her flipper as we body-surfed together.

She was a beautiful, green sea turtle, swimming free in the blue waters of Hawaii. She smiled at me and I knew she was happy. She was free. She was enjoying the salt water flowing over her shell and head.

She popped her head above water to make sure we were with her. Her eyes always watched us.

Grandmother was like a little kid. She, too, was diving and surfing in the waves.

She laughed out loud when waves washed over her. She looked like a young girl. She, too, was happy to be free in the water.

The moon had come up and gave Grandmother, Rocky Turtle, and me soft light to see.

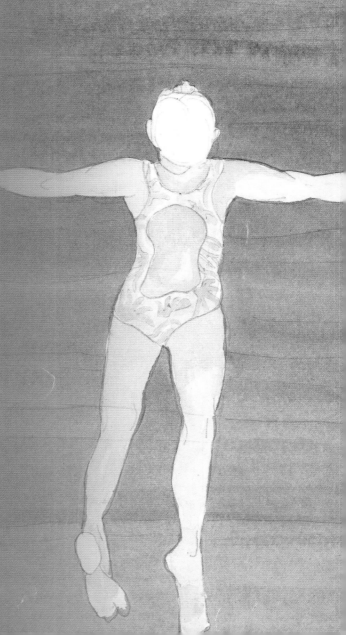

Facts Page

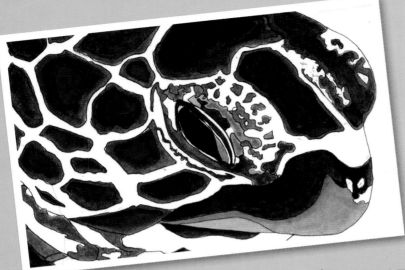

Green sea turtles are one of the largest sea turtles in the world. They can weigh up to 700 pounds and have a shell that measures 5 feet. Sea turtles existed before the dinosaurs! They have been on earth for more than 100 million years. Today they are endangered. That means that there aren't many left and they need our help to survive.

They aren't called green sea turtles because they are green. Their shells are actually brown or olive-green color. Adult green sea turtles are the only herbivorous sea turtle. That means they only eat plants. The fat in their body is green from all the algae plants they eat and the green fat gave them their name.

Sea turtles can live to be over 100 years old if they are lucky. Unlike turtles we see on land, sea turtles cannot pull their heads or flippers into their shells. Sea turtles face many challenges in the ocean. Their flippers or head can get tangled in fishing nets or fishing line. Fishing hooks can get stuck in their flippers. Boats can run over sea turtles, cutting their shell or flippers. And worse, humans hunt and capture sea turtles for their shells and meat.

Young sea turtles eat crabs, jellyfish, and sponges. If a plastic bag is floating in the ocean, they mistake it for jellyfish and eat it. The plastic bag makes young turtles sick and they can die. Adult sea turtles eat sea grasses and algae. They depend on us to keep the ocean clean so they have a large supply of food.

Sea turtles warm themselves by swimming in shallow water close to the surface. You can sometimes see them riding the waves. Occasionally, Hawaiian green sea turtles crawl ashore on the sandy beach. They may do this to warm up, rest, and sleep in the sun. Sometimes they do this to hide from tiger sharks who like to eat them!

Sea turtles are born in nests on the same beach where their mother was born. The female comes onto the beach to lay her eggs. Her instinct brings her back to the beach where she was born. At night, the female digs a nest in the ground with her back flippers. She lays 70-90 eggs the size of a ping pong ball and buries them in the nest, covering them with sand. She returns to the sea, leaving her eggs.

About two months later, the babies hatch out of the eggs, dig their way out of the nest, and move straight to the sea. Somehow they know they must live in the ocean and not on land. The trip to the ocean is very dangerous for the hatchlings as seagulls, crabs, reptiles, birds, and humans attack the baby turtles. Few live to adulthood.

The green sea turtle is significant in Hawaiian cultural history. In some creation myths, the world was created on the back of the turtle. Traditional Hawaiian management provided a buffer on the number of turtles harvested based on the kapu or taboo system. The legal killing of green sea turtles ended in 1978 when they were listed as threatened on the federal Endangered Species Act (ESA). Under this act, it is also illegal to harass, harm, harvest, or sell green sea turtles.

How can you help the sea turtles?

1) Keep the ocean free of trash and pollution.
2) When you walk the beach, pick up plastic bags, bottles, cups, food wrappers, and put them in garbage cans.
3) Do not leave fishing gear unattended.
4) If a sea turtle becomes entangled in your fishing gear, help to release it, and be sure to remove any trailing line.
5) If you see a honu in the wild, do not attempt to touch, grab, or feed it. This could cause distress to the turtle.
6) Tell your friends to help keep our oceans clean. Garbage and poisons in the ocean kill the food the turtles eat to survive.
7) You can help sea turtles by making a donation to the Hawaiian Wildlife Fund.

Tina Cole Kreitz was raised in the San Francisco Bay Area. For 37 years Tina was a teacher of at-risk children and co-director of a program for pregnant and parenting teens and their children. She enjoyed her job tremendously. Tina received many honors for her work and was inducted into the Woman's Hall of Fame as an outstanding educator. Tina's next career began in 2004 when she became a grandmother. Coming from a family of writers and storytellers made sharing tales with her grandchildren a tradition she enjoyed. When she retired from teaching, Tina focused on her writing and created stories incorporating her numerous travels with her husband, Bob. She developed new tales of adventure for her grandchildren. When not visiting new places, Tina is home in Alameda, California, where she is frequently seen bike riding and swimming with her children and grandchildren. Tina's next book will be an adventure story about a grandmother and her little puppet friend. The pair visit different locations around the world and write tales for the grandchildren at home in the USA.